Put Beginning Readers on the Right Track with ALL ABOARD READING™

The All Aboard Reading series is especially designed for beginning readers. Written by noted authors and illustrated in full color, these are books that children really want to read—books to excite their imagination, expand their interests, make them laugh, and support their feelings. With fiction and nonfiction stories that are high interest and curriculum-related, All Aboard Reading books offer something for every young reader. And with four different reading levels, the All Aboard Reading series lets you choose which books are most appropriate for your children and their growing abilities.

Picture Readers
Picture Readers have super-simple texts, with many nouns appearing as rebus pictures. At the end of each book are 24 flash cards—on one side is a rebus picture; on the other side is the written-out word.

Station Stop 1
Station Stop 1 books are best for children who have just begun to read. Simple words and big type make these early reading experiences more comfortable. Picture clues help children to figure out the words on the page. Lots of repetition throughout the text helps children to predict the next word or phrase—an essential step in developing word recognition.

Station Stop 2
Station Stop 2 books are written specifically for children who are reading with help. Short sentences make it easier for early readers to understand what they are reading. Simple plots and simple dialogue help children with reading comprehension.

Station Stop 3
Station Stop 3 books are perfect for children who are reading alone. With longer text and harder words, these books appeal to children who have mastered basic reading skills. More complex stories captivate children who are ready for more challenging books.

In addition to All Aboard Reading books, look for All Aboard Math Readers™ (fiction stories that teach math concepts children are learning in school); All Aboard Science Readers™ (nonfiction books that explore the most fascinating science topics in age-appropriate language); and All Aboard Poetry Readers™ (funny, rhyming poems for readers of all levels).

All Aboard for happy reading!

© 2004 The Wiggles Pty Ltd. U.S. Representative HIT Entertainment. All rights reserved. Published by Grosset & Dunlap, a division of Penguin Young Readers Group, 345 Hudson Street, New York, New York 10014. GROSSET & DUNLAP and ALL ABOARD READING are trademarks of Penguin Group (USA) Inc. Printed in the U.S.A.

Library of Congress Cataloging-in-Publication Data is available.

ISBN 0-448-43500-4   A B C D E F G H I J

ALL ABOARD READING™

Station Stop
1

Dorothy's Garden

Illustrated by Bob Berry

Grosset & Dunlap • New York

Dorothy the Dinosaur loved gardening. She liked digging, planting, watering, weeding, and picking pretty flowers.

SEEDS
SEE
SEE

Dorothy also knew that
planting seeds was hard work.

When it was warm enough
to plant the seedlings in her
garden, Dorothy invited The
Wiggles and Wags to help.

She showed them the seeds and
said, "Now you can plant them."
"Just show us what to do,"
Anthony said.

"First, we dig lots of holes,"
Dorothy began.
"I dig digging," laughed Jeff!

Everyone laughed
and began working.

When the digging was done, Dorothy said, "Put the seeds in the ground, then cover them all around."

Wags patted the ground
around each seedling
with his big, brown paws.
"That's very good!" Dorothy said.

"Now it's time to give the seedlings some water," Dorothy said.

The Wiggles and Wags sprinkled
water on the thirsty seedlings.
They were having so much fun
watering the seedlings that it took
them a while to notice someone
was missing.

Jeff had fallen asleep
among the violets.
Anthony, Murray, and
Greg watered Jeff along
with the seedlings.

Jeff rubbed his eyes and yawned.
Dorothy laughed. "Well, they are
called flower <u>beds</u>."

15

Dorothy looked around her garden. "Thank you all very much!" she exclaimed.

Anthony said, "It looks like a lot of mud."

Dorothy giggled. "Well, it does now, but wait until these flowers grow and bloom, bloom, BLOOM!"

To thank them for all their help,
Dorothy served a delicious
lunch of sandwiches and fruit.

Anthony rubbed his stomach.
"I think picnics are the best
thing about a garden."

Murray pointed to Jeff, who was snoring. He whispered, "Jeff thinks outdoor sleeping is the best thing about a garden."

Jeff stretched and yawned, then smiled. "Your garden is a great place to sleep," he told Dorothy.

Dorothy invited her other friends, Captain Feathersword and Henry the Octopus, to her garden.

"A garden is a great place to do lots of things," Captain Feathersword said. "Like play catch."

"A garden is also a great place to fly kites," said Henry the Octopus.

When it was time to go home,
Dorothy once again thanked
Wags and The Wiggles for
helping to plant her garden.
"It was fun!" Jeff said.
Greg grinned. "Yes, we all
had a very good time."

After a few weeks of watering
and weeding, Dorothy called
her friends. "I have a surprise
for you!" she exclaimed.

Everyone hurried to
Dorothy's house. She took
them into the garden.

Everywhere they looked there were beautiful flowers. Dorothy giggled. "I told you they were going to grow and bloom, bloom, BLOOM!"

Dorothy and her friends
spent a wonderful afternoon
picnicking and playing in
the flower-filled garden.

Dorothy the Dinosaur smiled and said, "The best thing about a garden is sharing it with friends."